BRO I'M STILL FIGURING IT OUT

REVANTH

ISBN
Paperback 979-8-89906-612-2
Hardcase 979-8-89961-340-1

Dedication

For the younger me, and anyone else who thought they had to have it all figured out by now.

Contents

Preface 7

About the Author 9

Prologue: The Week Everything Felt Off 11

PART I: FOGGY HEAD, HEAVY HEART

1. The Art of Shutting Down 17
2. When It All Fell Quiet. 25
3. The Test I Wasn't Ready For 35

PART II: THE UNRAVELLING

4. The Six-Mile Walk. .45
5. Breathing Underwater 53

PART III: FIGURING MYSELF OUT

6. Self-Doubt and Self-Acceptance 61
7. Things I Never Said to My Mom 85
8. The People Who See You Before You See
   Yourself. 95

9. Shortcut Season Is Over .109

10. Slow Wins, Soft Strength 115

PART IV: TURNING THE PAGE

11. I Didn't Mean to Start Anything 125

12. I'm Not Done Yet (But I'm Different Now). .133

Epilogue: Letter to My 13-Year-Old Self 139

Acknowledgements 143

Preface

I didn't sit down one day and decide to write a book. I just needed a place to pour out everything I was figuring out – the messy thoughts, the quiet wins, the things I didn't even know how to say out loud.

It started with random scribbles late at night. A few half-finished paragraphs. A few jokes I thought only I would find funny.

Somewhere along the way, it became something bigger — not because it's perfect, but because it's real.

This is a story about figuring it out, messing up, trying again, and slowly learning that maybe you don't have to have everything sorted out to be proud of where you are.

If you're someone who's still figuring yourself out, welcome. You're exactly where you need to be.

About the Author

Revanth is a 16-year-old student who never imagined he'd write a book—until one day, a bunch of midnight scribbles turned into something more. Between school, college prep, and figuring out life one messy chapter at a time, he discovered that writing helped him process everything he couldn't always say out loud. *Bro, I'm Still Figuring Out* is his first book—real, reflective, and straight from the voice of a teen still figuring things out (but getting better at it every day).

He hopes other teens will find bits of themselves in these pages—and maybe, just maybe, feel a little more seen.

The Week Everything Felt Off

If you had asked me a few months ago what I was going on with me, I'd probably have said something like, "Nothing much. Just school and stuff."

And honestly, I would've believed it at that time. I didn't even know what I wanted to do with my life. Apart from just being myself, playing video games, hanging out with friends, eating my favourite food, sleeping, and studying—I didn't think much beyond that.

Because that's what I used to do—brush things off. Play it cool. Pretend everything was fine even when something deep down felt... off.

It wasn't one big thing that messed with me. It was a bunch of little ones that all happened in the same week.

I bombed a mock maths test I thought I was ready for.

I got into a stupid fight with my closest friends and ended up getting ghosted from the group chat.

And at home? I just didn't want to talk. Not to my mom. Not to anyone.

I don't know what shifted exactly, but that week made everything feel louder—my thoughts, my moods, my frustration. And instead of talking about it (which, let's be honest, wasn't happening), I opened my laptop and started typing.

Not to write a book.

Not to share anything with anyone.

Just... to dump it all somewhere outside my head.

The self-doubt, the frustration, the low confidence, the anger – it all began to pour out through my words.

It wasn't neat. It wasn't even clear what I was writing at first. But as I kept going, I started noticing patterns. Things I'd never said out loud before. Stuff I didn't even realise was bothering me. It all just started spilling out—messy, weird, kind of embarrassing, but also kind of real.

And the more I wrote, the more it made sense.

Not just the things that happened that week, but the stuff I'd been carrying for way longer than I thought.

So yeah... this wasn't supposed to be a book. It was supposed to be a vent session.

But maybe, somewhere in all that noise, I started to figure things out.

Not everything. But enough.

This is the story of how that happened.

HARPPO

Part 1

Foggy Head, Heavy Heart

(When everything starts to feel off,
but you don't know why.)

Chapter 1

The Art of Shutting Down

For as long as I can remember, I've been pretty good at pretending everything's fine. I don't remember when it started exactly, but I was old enough to have opinions and young enough to believe that life was just about school, games, and having fun. And anything negative—I'd brush it off like it didn't matter.

Not in some dramatic, fake-it-till-you-make-it way. More like, if I don't talk about what's bothering me, maybe it'll go away on its own. Or at least shrink down into something small enough to ignore. I don't know when that became my go-to, but it did. Somewhere between middle school and now, I turned into this expert at brushing things off and changing the topic when something got too real.

My mom used to ask me questions all the time. Not in an annoying way—well, okay, sometimes it was annoying—but mostly just her trying to check in. Things like, "How was your day?" or "You seemed quiet at dinner, what's up?" And for a long time, I answered with the same stuff: "Nothing." "I'm fine." "Just tired."

It's weird because, in the beginning, I think I actually wanted her to push back. Like, to ask again or dig a little deeper. But she didn't. She took the hint. Eventually, the questions stopped coming as often. She'd still watch me like she could hear the things I wasn't saying, but she backed off. And I told myself that was a good thing—that now I had the space I wanted.

But here's the thing about space: it feels great until it doesn't.

At first, it was nice. No one hovering. No one asking for explanations I didn't feel like giving. I could go to my room, close the door, and stay in my bubble. Headphones on, lights off, Netflix or music or whatever playing loud enough to drown out any thoughts trying to sneak in. And for a while, it worked. I felt in control.

But then came that week—the one where everything just got… heavy. The math test. The friend group drama. The silence at home that started feeling a little too quiet. I found myself lying on my bed one evening, phone face down, staring at the ceiling like it held answers. I wasn't sad exactly, and I wasn't angry either.

It was more like everything inside me had hit pause. I didn't feel like doing anything. Not gaming. Not texting. Not even eating, which for me is a sign something's seriously off.

I remember my mom knocked on the door and asked if I was okay. I said I had a headache. That was a lie. I just didn't feel like talking. She paused outside for a second and then walked away without saying anything else. And, for some reason, that bugged me. I wanted her to stay. But also, I didn't.

That's the part I don't know how to explain. I wanted to be left alone, but also not completely alone. I wanted someone to understand me without me having to explain anything. Which I know sounds impossible, but that's how it felt. Like I didn't have the energy to talk about what was wrong, but I still wanted someone to know that it was.

That was probably when I realised I'd been doing this thing for a long time—this shutting down thing. It had become automatic.

Something annoyed me? Shut down.

Someone disappointed me? Shut down.

School felt overwhelming? Shut down.

It was like I had this invisible switch that I could flick to "off" whenever I didn't want to deal with something. And I convinced myself it made me stronger, like I was in control.

But during that week, the switch wasn't doing much. I'd flick it, and the feelings stayed. I couldn't block them out the way I used to. They just sat there, like background noise I couldn't mute. And what's worse is, I didn't even know what exactly I was feeling. It was a mix of everything—frustration, disappointment, loneliness, and a weird kind of guilt that I didn't know how to name.

I think part of the guilt came from how I'd handled things with my friends. The fight wasn't even that dramatic. It started with a joke that went too far, then a group call that I wasn't invited to, and then suddenly, I wasn't being replied to at all. The usual stuff that teenagers probably go through, but when you're in it, it feels personal. I tried acting like I didn't care. Laughed it off in front of other people. Scrolled past their posts, pretending it didn't sting. But deep down, I was pissed. And I didn't know what to do with that feeling.

I didn't want to talk to anyone about it because I was embarrassed. Like, what was I even supposed to say? "Hey, my friends are being jerks, and I feel left out"? That felt lame. Weak. So instead, I did what I always do—kept it to myself.

Same with the test. I had convinced myself I could handle it with my usual last-minute prep and a few YouTube shortcuts. When the results came in, and I saw how badly I'd done, I told everyone it was just a mock, didn't count, no big deal. But it didn't feel like no big deal. It felt like maybe I wasn't as good at faking it as I thought. Like the version of me I'd built—laid-back, unbothered, just coasting—was starting to crack.

That night, I opened my laptop, stared at the blinking cursor for a few minutes, and started typing. I didn't have a plan. I wasn't trying to be deep or write anything meaningful. I just needed to get stuff out of my head. I wrote about the test, the fight, the silence at home. I wrote about how I missed the way things used to be with my mom, even though I was the one who had pushed her away. I wrote about how tired I was of pretending like I was okay all the time.

It wasn't clean, structured, or even fully coherent. But once I started, I couldn't stop. And for the first time in a while, I felt like I wasn't bottling everything up. I wasn't solving anything, but at least I was looking at it instead of avoiding it.

That night didn't change my life. But it cracked something open.

I wish I could say I woke up the next morning with some big revelation or that I apologised to everyone and fixed everything. I didn't. I still ghosted texts. Still zoned out in class. Still avoided eye contact at the dinner table. But I also kept writing. Not every day. Not with any real plan. Just when I needed to. And each time, I understood myself a little better.

I started to notice patterns. Like how I only ever shut down around people I actually cared about. Like how pretending to be unbothered took more energy than just admitting I was hurt. Like how space is only helpful if you use it to breathe, not to build walls.

Looking back, I don't think shutting down makes you strong. I think it makes you stuck. And I was stuck for a long time.

This chapter doesn't end with a solution. There's no "here's what to do instead" section. Because I'm still figuring that part out. What I do know is that bottling things up only works for so long. At some point, the pressure builds. And when it does, it's better to have a way out than to keep holding it in and hoping nobody notices.

So this is me - noticing it.

And maybe that's the first step.

Chapter 2

When It All Fell Quiet

The weirdest part wasn't the fight. It was the silence that came after.

You always expect the shouting, the swearing, the full-blown "I'm done with you" moment. But that's not how it happened. One day, we were laughing about the dumbest memes on the group chat, and the next, I was staring at my phone, wondering why no one was responding.

It started with something small. It always does. A joke that went too far—directed at me this time. Normally, I'd laugh it off or throw something back, but that day I didn't. Maybe because I was already dealing with too much, or maybe because it wasn't actually funny. I said, "That was kinda messed up," in the chat, and then everything just... shifted. The energy changed. The messages slowed. A few passive-aggressive replies. Then nothing.

At first, I figured they were just busy. But then I saw they were online. Then I saw their stories—hanging out, tagging each other, inside jokes that clearly didn't include me.

And that's when I realised: I was on the outside now.

It wasn't official. No one told me I was out. But that's the thing about being shut out – you don't always hear the door slam. Sometimes you just look around and notice you're not in the room anymore.

I didn't want to admit how much it bothered me. Even to myself. These were my good friends. People I'd known since early school. People who had seen me in my cringiest, most awkward stages. And just like that, it felt like they had voted me off the island and moved on.

I kept checking my phone like a glitchy app. Maybe I missed something. Maybe there was a message coming that would explain everything, clear it up, or just… undo it.

But it stayed quiet.

At school, I tried to play it cool. I sat with different people. Laughed a little louder to make it seem like I was fine. I told myself I needed new friends anyway. That they were immature. That I didn't need them.

And at home, everything was quiet too. Not in a dramatic way. My mom and I still exchanged the usual stuff—"Are you hungry?" "Did you pack your bag?" "What time is your class?" —but the real conversations had gone missing. I didn't tell her about what was happening. I didn't want to deal with the look she gives when she knows something's wrong but also knows I won't talk about it.

So instead, I kept acting like nothing was different. Except now, even when I was surrounded by people, I felt like I was in some kind of invisible box. Like I was there, but not really.

The thing about silence is that, after a while, it starts talking to you. You start hearing thoughts you didn't know you had. Questions like: Was I being too sensitive? Did I overreact? Were they ever really my friends, or was I just a convenient part of the group?

It's not that I hadn't had fights with friends before. But this one felt different. Not because of how it happened, but because of when. It came at a time when everything else in my life already felt shaky. Like the test, the pressure, the way I'd been feeling in general—this just pushed it all over the edge.

And the worst part? I didn't know how to fix it.

Not just the friendship, but myself in the middle of all of it.

I didn't reach out to them. Not because I didn't want to—but because I didn't know what I'd even say. "Hey, can we not be weird anymore?" sounded stupid. "I miss you guys" felt too honest. And "Let's talk" was way too vulnerable. So I said nothing.

And they said nothing in return.

I kept it all inside for a while. But one night, lying in bed, I started typing again. Just dumping everything I wanted to say but couldn't. I wrote a message I never sent. Something like:

"I don't know why things got weird. I miss the way it used to be. If I said something that messed things up, I didn't mean to. I was just tired. I was going through stuff. But I still thought we were good. I still thought you were my people."

I sat there staring at it for a long time.

I didn't send it.

Not because I was angry, but because I didn't know if I'd be able to handle being ignored again. That felt scarier than staying silent.

So I closed the chat, opened my Notes app, and dropped the message in there like a letter to no one. I figured maybe one day I'd come back to it. Or maybe I wouldn't. But at least it wasn't sitting inside me anymore, buzzing like a phone you've left on vibrate.

There's something really strange about realising you don't have the people you thought would always be there. It makes you rethink a lot. Not just about them, but about who you are without them. When your routine doesn't involve that group chat, those after-school meetups, or the jokes only you understood—it leaves a weird blank space you don't know how to fill.

For a while, I tried to replace it. I hung out more with this other group. They were cool, but I didn't feel like I could really let my guard down around them. I wasn't the version of myself I used to be. I was quieter, a little more careful. Like I was waiting to see if they'd ghost me too.

Looking back, I think that stretch of time taught me more than any big dramatic moment ever could. It taught me how much I'd let my identity be shaped by the people around me. How I measured my worth by the responses I got in a chat, or the invites to hang out, or the laughter in a group. And when all that disappeared, I didn't know where that left me.

That's a terrifying place to be in at 16. When the people you've grown up with suddenly feel like strangers, and you're left trying to figure out if it's them who changed or if it's you.

Maybe it's both.

But here's what I've learned—not in a perfect, I-have-it-all-figured-out way, but just from sitting with that blank space: sometimes silence is the universe's way of telling you to listen to yourself for a change.

Because once I stopped trying to fill the quiet with noise or distractions, I started hearing things I hadn't paid attention to in a long time.

What I liked. What I missed. What I needed.

And while I was dealing with all this silent drama—inside my head and outside of it—school was buzzing in a whole different way.

Everyone suddenly seemed to be planning their future.

Which subjects to take.

Which undergrad to aim for.

What career sounded "cool enough" to say out loud in front of teachers and parents.

The same group chats that once shared memes were now filled with college info dumps, SAT tips, subject comparisons, and talk about career counsellors.

And me? I was still figuring out how to even feel normal again.

But watching everyone get so serious about their future… made me pause.

Not in a "oh no, I'm behind" kind of way. More like—what am I doing?

That's when I started thinking about what I actually enjoyed. What made me feel like I had some sort of control over my own story.

I was like any other normal kid—I didn't know exactly what I wanted to become.

But I knew this:

I wanted to do well in life.

I just wanted to be happy.

Figure things out on my own terms.

I liked maths. It felt solid. Numbers excited me. It came very naturally to me.

Business sounded fun.

Finance was another word I kept hearing. I thought investment banking sounded cool— something about markets and money felt powerful and kind of exciting.

But then came the chaos.

The pressure.

The noise.

That's when my mom—who saw me overwhelmed—quietly signed me up with a counsellor.

At first, I thought, "Do I really need this?"

But after a few weeks, I started realising something…

I didn't need to chase everything. I just needed to figure out what I was good at—and stick with that.

I wasn't a topper. I wasn't struggling. I was good and steady. So I leaned into that.

I still don't know if those friendships are fixable. Maybe they are. Maybe they're not. But I've stopped waiting for someone else to unmute me. I've started choosing who I want to be when no one else is watching.

And that, surprisingly, feels kind of freeing. That's when everything started to shift.

Chapter 3

The Test I Wasn't Ready For

I've always had this unspoken thing with school: if I didn't try too hard, then failure didn't really count.

Like, if I studied for a test and still bombed it, that would suck. But if I barely prepared and did okay, I could just shrug and say, "I didn't even try." Somehow, that made me feel like I had the upper hand. Like I was in control.

It's a weird kind of logic, but I know a lot of people who think like that. Keep expectations low. Coast a little. Don't look like you're trying too hard. Especially if you're usually known as one of the "smart" kids—then it's even more tempting to pretend like good marks just happen by accident.

And for a while, they did. I mean, not by magic or anything, but I had my systems. Crash courses on YouTube, notes from friends, late-night speed-reading sessions. It worked well enough. I wasn't topping the class or anything, but I wasn't struggling either.

Until math.

Math didn't care about my systems. Math wanted attention. Repetition. Focus. Things I wasn't used to giving.

There was a time when I thought I had hacked the system—especially when it came to school. I was the kind of kid who did just enough and still got by. I was one of those students who could "read" maths like a storybook and still score very well.

Why bother solving 10 problems when you can understand the method once and wing the rest?

Why revise the full chapter when there's a beautifully packaged YouTube shortcut telling you "everything you need to know"?

No deep practice. Just reading through concepts, solving 3-4 sample sums, and walking into the exam.

It worked. Until it didn't.

Until Grade 10, that strategy got me consistency.

As maths and I? We were cool.

But then Grade 11 happened. Deeper subjects. Tougher papers. More pressure.

And boom - The mock exam came right in the middle of all the other chaos. I told myself I'd study properly for it. That I'd finally put in the effort, get serious, turn things around. I even printed out the syllabus and highlighted chapters. That was the extent of my preparation. Highlighting.

I remember walking into the exam room that morning feeling tired but weirdly confident. Like maybe I'd just absorbed enough over time to survive it. The first few questions weren't bad. I scribbled fast, skipped the hard ones, and told myself I'd come back to them.

By the halfway mark, I was stuck.

Not just stuck – I was blank.

Looking at the paper felt like trying to read in a different language. The numbers didn't form anything meaningful. I reread one question five times and still didn't understand what it was asking.

My brain, which normally has at least *something* to say, was silent. Like it had decided to walk out and let me deal with the mess.

That was the first time I remember feeling genuinely panicked during a test. Not "oh no, I forgot this formula" panic, but the kind that makes your heart race and your hands go cold. I couldn't focus. Couldn't think. I started doodling in the margin of the question paper just to keep my hand moving.

When the bell rang, I handed in my paper without looking at anyone. The walk home felt like moving through a tunnel – no sound, no light, just the thudding reminder that I'd completely, absolutely failed.

I didn't tell anyone how bad it went. When my mom asked, I gave the usual "It was alright" and went straight to my room. I wasn't ready for the conversation. Not because she'd be mad, but because I didn't want to say out loud what I was already thinking: maybe I wasn't actually good at this. Maybe I'd just been lucky all along.

The results came a week later. I didn't even have to look. My teacher placed the paper on my desk face down with that expression that said, "We'll talk later." I waited until break time, then flipped it open.

29%. For someone who is always used to seeing 85% above with little practice, and now seeing 29%, as per me, was very bad.

There was a moment—like five seconds—where my brain tried to come up with excuses. Maybe she marked it too harshly. Maybe they made a mistake. Maybe everyone did badly. But I knew the truth.

I bombed it because I wasn't ready. Not mentally. Not emotionally. And definitely not in terms of actual maths prep.

The shame didn't hit all at once. It crept in slowly, over the next few days. Every time someone mentioned the mock scores. Every time I avoided looking at my teacher in class. Every time I watched my friends exchange notes and realised I had nothing to contribute.

I started feeling like a fake. Like this whole laid-back, "I don't need to try" thing was just a cover. And now that it wasn't working, I didn't know who I was underneath it.

Eventually, I had to tell my mom. Not because she found out—she didn't push—but because I couldn't carry it alone anymore. I told her over dinner. Kind of mumbled it between bites of rice.

She didn't react the way I expected. No lectures. No disappointment. She just nodded and asked, "So what now?"

That question stuck with me. Not "Why did this happen?" or "What were you thinking?" Just: what now? For the first time, I had to answer that for myself.

I thought about pretending it didn't matter, about moving on to the next thing and hoping for better luck. But that didn't feel right anymore. I didn't want to feel this helpless again. I didn't want to keep bluffing my way through school like some magician with one trick left.

So I made a decision I never thought I'd make. I asked if I could delay my maths exam. Just by a few weeks. Enough time to actually prepare. Properly, this time.

I needed practice and in-depth learning to score an A* —and that couldn't come with shortcuts. While many of my classmates wrote their current maths exam in February, I moved mine to June.

It wasn't an easy decision.

It wasn't some grand moment of turning my life around. I didn't suddenly become obsessed with studying. But I started small. One chapter at a time. Writing things down. Watching the videos twice instead of just skimming the comments. Asking questions even when I felt stupid.

The first few days were rough. I kept getting distracted. I'd sit down with the best intentions and end up on Reddit reading about why humans invented zero. But I kept showing up. That was the main difference.

What surprised me wasn't how much I learned, but how it made me feel. Not proud. Not smart. Just… stable. Like I was finally building something real instead of pretending I already had.

My mom had been saying this to me for months: "Maths can't be read like a novel. You have to practice."

Of course, I ignored her. In my mind, she didn't get the "new system." She didn't understand how we study these days. There were days I snapped at her. I told her she was "out of touch."

That she shouldn't interfere because she couldn't even solve my Grade 10 problems.

She wasn't mad. But I could tell she was hurt. And yet, she kept showing up. She paid my maths exam fee twice. She sat with me even when she didn't know the answers.

My 11th-grade maths exam is just a few months away. Yes, I'm in 12th now.

Yes, my friends finished theirs in February. But I'm okay with that.

Because this journey – of choosing effort over shortcuts – has taught me more than any formula ever could. And honestly? Writing has been therapy.

It's helped me reflect.

It's helped me finally say things out loud:

I think we spend so much time trying to avoid failure that we forget it's actually a really useful signal. It doesn't mean you suck. It means the way you've been doing things might not be working anymore.

That maths test didn't ruin my life. But it broke the version of me that thought he didn't need to care.

And maybe that was the point.

Part 2

The Unravelling

(When things that were bottled up start spilling out.)

Chapter 4

The Six-Mile Walk

The trip to London was supposed to be a break. My mom thought a change of scenery would do me good. Get me out of my head for a bit. Give us both something different to focus on. She was probably right—but at that point, I wasn't really in the mood to be around anyone, especially her.

We stayed with cousins. The kind of family that's always cheerful and ready with an itinerary. On the first day, they planned a full schedule: brunch at some place with overpriced toast, a visit to the Natural History Museum, and a walk along the Thames. All very Instagram-friendly.

I was there, physically. I smiled when people pointed cameras at me. I said "cool", "nice", and "looks good" on repeat. But inside, I still felt heavy—like I'd brought all the stuff I was trying to get away from packed into an invisible suitcase. Same thoughts, same guilt, same stuck feeling. Just now with different weather.

On the third day, we were walking through this massive park—Hyde Park, I think—when something just snapped. It wasn't dramatic. I didn't yell or storm off. I just slowed down, let everyone get a little ahead of me, and then told my mom I was heading back to the hotel early.

She looked at me for a second, like she wanted to say something, but then just nodded and said, "Text me when you get there."

I didn't take the train or an Uber. I didn't even open Google Maps for directions. I just started walking.

At first, it was just about putting distance between me and everything else. I wasn't thinking big thoughts or trying to find myself or whatever. I just didn't want to be around people. My brain felt like one of those tabs on a laptop that's frozen and won't close. I couldn't figure out what I needed, so I just moved my body instead.

The thing about walking in a city that's not yours is you notice everything. The little things. A guy feeding pigeons with way too much enthusiasm. A couple arguing in low voices. A kid riding a scooter and nearly crashing into a bench. It all becomes part of this blurry background that's way more interesting than your own thoughts, which, if you're lucky, gets a little quieter as you go.

I kept walking. Past coffee shops, through another park, across a bridge. I didn't count steps or time. I didn't care where I was headed. I just kept going.

Somewhere around mile four—though I didn't know that at the time—my legs started to ache. Not in a bad way. More like they were reminding me I was still here, still moving. And something in me started to settle. I didn't feel lighter, exactly. But I felt… emptied out. Like some of the pressure inside had finally leaked out onto the pavement behind me.

I sat down on a bench near a fountain. The kind of bench you see in movies when someone needs a moment of reflection. It was probably meant for old people resting their knees, but that day, it felt like it had been waiting for me.

I didn't do anything profound. I didn't cry or have a flash of insight. I just took off my jacket, drank from a bottle of water I didn't realise I'd been holding, and let my mind wander.

And that's when the question hit me—not like a bolt of lightning or some life-changing epiphany, but quietly, in the background of my thoughts: *What are you actually running from?*

Because that's what it felt like. Not a walk. A low-key escape.

Not from the park or the cousins or even the awkward energy with my mom. But from everything piling up inside me. From being the guy who always says, "I'm good." From the guilt of failing. From the awkward space that opened up when my friends went silent. From the weird, floaty feeling of not knowing where I stood with anyone anymore—not even myself.

And in that moment, sitting there on that ugly metal bench with sore feet and a hoodie that smelled like aeroplane air, I realised something:

I didn't hate myself. I wasn't broken. I was just overwhelmed. And I had no idea how to say that to anyone. Including me.

Back home, everything had started to blur together—school, emotions, pressure, silence. It was like every part of my life was competing for my attention, and none of it made sense. But here, in a place that didn't ask anything from me, I could finally feel all of it without trying to fix any of it.

After maybe 20 minutes, I got up again. I thought about calling my mom to let her know I was fine, but I didn't. Not because I didn't care, but because I knew if I heard her voice, I'd lose the quiet I had just found. I'd go back into defence mode. I'd say, "Yeah, I'm good", even if I wasn't ready to pretend yet.

So I walked some more. My feet hurt. My phone battery was low. I still didn't use Maps. I figured I'd recognise something eventually.

By the time I reached the hotel, it was dark. I stopped at a vending machine in the lobby and bought a Coke – not because I wanted one, but because it felt like the kind of thing someone would do in a coming-of-age movie. Sit down. Open a Coke. Take a breath.

That night, I didn't write anything. I didn't unpack the walk in my Notes app or try to turn it into a lesson. I just lay in bed and let the soreness in my legs remind me that I had walked through something— not just across the city, but through the fog in my own head.

The next morning, my mom didn't say anything about the night before. She just handed me a breakfast plate and sat next to me while we watched TV. Some British quiz show with too many rules. I didn't say much either. But the silence between us felt different. Not tense. Just there. Like we both understood something without needing to talk about it.

It took me a while to figure out what that walk actually meant. At the time, it just felt necessary. Like if I didn't move, I'd snap. But later, when I thought about it—and yeah, I did end up writing about it—I realised something I hadn't seen before.

When everything feels out of control—your grades, your friendships, your own thoughts—moving your body is a way of reminding yourself that *you* still have a say. Even if it's just choosing which direction to go. Even if it's just walking until your brain gets tired of yelling.

It didn't fix anything, that walk. My grades didn't suddenly bounce back. My friends didn't text with a dramatic apology. I didn't wake up the next day with some newfound purpose.

But I felt clearer.

Not fixed. Not happy. Just... not spinning anymore.

Sometimes you don't need a solution. You just need a little space to catch your breath and let your thoughts stretch their legs.

That walk was mine.

Chapter 5

Breathing Underwater

I've never liked water. Not showers. Not pools. Definitely not the ocean.

It's not like I had some traumatic experience as a kid. No horror story involving a pool cover or a near-drowning moment. It was just a constant, low-level fear—this sense that water had a mind of its own and I didn't belong in it. I hated not being able to see what was below. I hated the feeling of my breath getting short. I hated how people looked so relaxed while I was panicking under the surface like some badly programmed video game character.

But because I never said any of that out loud, people just assumed I was indifferent. Friends would jump into the pool at parties and yell for me to join. I'd laugh and wave it off like I was too cool to care. "Nah, I'll just chill on the side." Inside, my heart would be racing even watching them splash around.

We landed in the Andamans for a holiday with my friends and family… and I still had the tension of fear-of-water thing amongst everything else…

The island was beautiful, like one of those places you'd see on a postcard and assume was photoshopped. Blue water that didn't even look real. Sand so white it made your shoes look offensive. My cousins were buzzing with excitement, already planning scuba dives and boat rides. I was planning how to get out of all of it without looking like a coward.

But then something strange happened. One of them—my old-time friend—turned to me during lunch and said, "You should try diving. It's not as scary as it looks."

Me? In the ocean? When I can barely handle a swimming pool? No way! But a part of me wanted to say yes. I wanted to see what would happen if I stopped running from fear. So, I disconcertedly said, "Yeah, maybe." It wasn't a real commitment. Just a maybe. But everyone latched onto it. The next day, we were signed up for a beginner's scuba dive. No turning back.

The morning of the dive, I woke up with that kind of nervous energy that makes you want to throw up and run away at the same time. I kept thinking about excuses. A stomach ache. A fever. I even checked my own temperature with the back of my hand like that would make it real.

But I didn't say anything. I got dressed. I went.

The dive centre was a tiny hut near the beach, with wetsuits hanging like limp shadows on a rack. The instructor was this chill guy named Anand, who had been diving for something like 20 years. He explained everything slowly, clearly, like we were five years old. Breathe through your mouth. Equalise the pressure in your ears. Don't panic if your mask fills with water.

All I heard was: you might panic, and your mask might fill with water.

They had us practice in the shallow bit first. Just kneel underwater and breathe through the regulator. Simple enough. Except my brain wasn't convinced. The minute my head went underwater, my instincts kicked in like alarms. Every part of my body screamed to get out. Everything terrified me - the weight of the oxygen tank, the tightness of the mask, the thought of forgetting how to communicate underwater, the possibility of a shark appearing out of nowhere!

I shot back up and yanked the mouthpiece out like I'd just swallowed a bee. Anand didn't say anything. He just nodded and said, "Take your time."

Everyone else looked fine. Comfortable, even. Floating like it was second nature. I stood there on the edge, dripping and shaking a little, trying not to let anyone see how badly I wanted to quit.

But then I thought about that moment on the bench in Hyde Park. The one where I realised I wasn't broken—I was just overwhelmed. That came back to me now. This was the same feeling. Not failure. Just fear. And maybe fear didn't always mean stop.

So I tried again.

This time, I just focused on breathing. I let myself sink slowly, kneeling in the shallows, water up to my chin, then over my head. My hands were clenched into fists. My brain still felt jumpy. But I was doing it. Sort of.

Eventually, we moved out to the dive site. A boat ride away, deeper water. I didn't talk much on the ride. Just stared out at the horizon like it might give me a reason to bail. It didn't.

We suited up, strapped on tanks, and sat on the edge of the boat like we were in some action movie. Anand gave us the final signal and said, "You'll be fine. Just remember to breathe."

I went last.

The water was warm but still made me flinch when I hit it. For a second, I forgot everything. Then the regulator kicked in. I breathed. Not calmly, but enough.

As we sank, the world shifted. I felt the water wrapped around me in a way I had never experienced before. Sounds disappeared. Colours deepened. Everything slowed down. It was like entering a new dimension—one where everything obeyed different rules. I held onto the instructor's arm like a toddler in a crowd, but I was underwater. Fully under. And breathing. I could hear nothing but my own breathing. It felt like the water wasn't my enemy anymore. It was calm, peaceful, beautiful!

I looked around and saw schools of fish weaving through coral, sunlight cutting through the water in golden beams, and the endless blue stretching all around me. By now, I felt I wasn't just tolerating the water; I was embracing it.

About ten minutes in, I felt something shift inside me. I felt a little less on edge. I let go of Anand's arm. I was hovering close to him, but being on my own. I wasn't thinking about grades, friends, or whether I looked stupid in a wetsuit. I was just there. Floating. Breathing. Existing without fear, even if it was just for a while.

When we came back up, I pulled off the mask and gasped—not because I needed air, but because I had done it. I didn't smile. I didn't cheer. I just blinked at the sky and felt something inside me unclench.

Later that night, lying in bed, I kept thinking about what that dive meant. The whole incident felt like proof to me that fear doesn't always mean danger. Fear isn't real – it's just a mental wall we build over time. And maybe the only way to break that wall is to face it head-on. The things we fear the most can sometimes be the biggest reasons for our personal growth!

Part 3

Figuring Myself Out

(Not fixed, not perfect – just more aware.)

Chapter 6

Self-Doubt and Self-Acceptance

If you had asked me a few years back, "Hey, are you confident?" I would've probably grinned, shrugged, and thrown out a "Yeah, bro, obviously."

But inside? That answer wasn't so obvious.

It never was.

For as long as I can remember, I've struggled with this weird, uncomfortable feeling that maybe I wasn't *really* there. The weird background feeling buzzing under everything—this little whisper that maybe, just maybe, I am not enough. It wasn't anything dramatic. No public humiliation. Not that I was bullied or anything big like that. It was quieter than that. It was more like... this slow, sneaky feeling that crept in. It was that feeling where you're with a group and you second-guess whether you should even say something. That feeling where you crack a joke and immediately wonder if it was dumb.

That feeling where you walk into a new place and your brain screams, "Bro, don't mess up, don't mess up."

Nor the feeling that maybe I wasn't cool enough. Or loud enough. Or interesting enough to be one of those people who just naturally belonged.

It showed up in small ways first. Like hesitating to speak up when a group was laughing and chatting — wondering if what I had to say was even worth saying in a large audience. Like feeling awkward during new class introductions or at birthday parties where I barely knew anyone. Like overthinking every "hi" and "what's up," making it seem ten times harder than it needed to be.

Making friends?

Bro, making friends sometimes felt like trying to solve a puzzle when half the pieces were missing. And you didn't even know what the final picture was supposed to look like.

You keep trying to fit yourself into spaces, hoping it clicks... but it doesn't.

Not fully.

Looking back, I think a lot of this started when we moved houses when I was a toddler.

Something that sounds so casual when you say it out loud— "Oh, we just shifted to a new place"—but when you're the kid inside that move?

It feels like someone picked up your entire world, shook it like a snow globe, and dropped you somewhere new... except now you have no map.

Before the Move – My Little World

Before everything shifted, before self-doubt even knew my name, there was this beautiful little world where I belonged without trying. We lived in a tiny apartment building, tucked away in a quiet lane that always smelled faintly of rain-soaked mud and roadside food.

The kind of place that felt like a pocket of magic in a giant, overwhelming world.

Our building wasn't anything fancy.

The walls were cracked.

The paint was peeling in places.

The lift made weird noises that made you wonder if today was the day it would finally give up.

The staircase always had chalk marks from kids playing tic-tac-toe and hopscotch.

The water sometimes shut off randomly mid-bath.

No generator when the power went out, and we ran outside and had dinner together under the candles.

The staircase always had chalk marks from kids playing tic-tac-toe and hopscotch.

Corridors were too huge to play four pillars, kick scooter, practice skating.

But to me, it was perfect then… It was home.

I had my small gang — four of us — thick as thieves.

We didn't need theme parks or giant malls to have fun.

We had the open sky, dusty roads, some cycles, a bat, and a tennis ball—that was enough to build kingdoms, battle monsters, and chase our imaginations.

Every evening, like clockwork, we would pour out of our houses full of energy and half-finished homework, and hearts full of excitement.

Nature was our playground.

The world outside was our gaming zone.

There was a patch of land right next to the building—full of sand—the house was being constructed—a good playground to climb up the sand pit and fall down.

Another patch nearby - There was this patch of wild land next to our building. It wasn't even a proper park—more like an abandoned plot with knee-high grass, random rocks, and weird noises that made it feel haunted at night.

That was our cricket ground.

Our football field.

Our WWE arena when we got bored and decided to wrestle.

We played 100-run cricket matches there, shouting fake commentary as if we were playing for India in a World Cup final.

We didn't care if the ball was old or the bat was cracked or the ground was half mud, half grass.

We didn't care if we fell, if we got bruised, if we got screamed at by angry aunties whose plants we accidentally smashed.

The rule was simple – if you hit the ball into the auntie's balcony, automatic out.

The ball rolling into the bushes meant a whole rescue operation, complete with "Be careful, there might be snakes!" warnings that made it ten times more thrilling.

We just played. And played. And played.

And came back home just to eat and sleep.

And just do my one-page homework at the max 😊

Learning to cycle was a full community event. I still remember the first time I balanced without support — wobbly, terrified, but flying.

The cheers that went up from the other kids made me feel like I had just won an Olympic medal.

And bro, that feeling — the rush, the pride, the freedom of wind against your face as you zoom past your friends, laughing so hard you can barely breathe — there's nothing in the world like it. Nothing.

Our gang included some honorary members too.

The street dogs around our building were like family.

Each one had a name we gave them — Bruno, Rocky, Chiku, Simba.

They knew us, and we knew them.

They sat with us on lazy Sunday afternoons when we'd lie on the road staring at the clouds, imagining what shapes we saw.

They would chase after our cycles, bark excitedly during our cricket matches, and curl up next to us when we sat gossiping on the roadside kerb, sipping on cold Maaza bottles we bought for 15 rupees from the little corner shop that smelled like spices and dusty candy jars.

That shop — bro, that was the hangout.

The aunty behind the counter knew us by name.

Bro, with 20 bucks, you were a king.

Maaza bottles sweating in the fridge, packets of Lays for ten bucks, Melody chocolates, those fizzy orange candies that made your tongue tingle.

We'd walk in like rockstars and walk out with treasures.

The aunty behind the counter knew all our names, our parents, our exam dates, everything.

We would raid the shelves for Maaza, Pepsi, Melody chocolates, and those colourful Rs. 5 toffees that somehow made us feel like billionaires.

Pocket money wasn't just money back then — it was dreams in coins.

And oh, Holi.

Our Holi wasn't the Instagram-filtered, neatly organised kind.

It was chaos.

It was buckets of water being thrown off terraces.

It was water balloons flying through the air like missiles.

It was chasing each other with fists full of bright powdered colours, painting each other's faces till we were unrecognisable — and laughing so hard our stomachs hurt.

It was the sound of music blasting from a cracked speaker somewhere, mixed with the shrieks and giggles of kids who didn't care about anything except living that moment fully.

Everything was loud.

Everything was messy.

Everything was so beautifully, heartbreakingly real.

No masks.

No filters.

No trying to be someone you weren't.

We didn't care if our clothes were torn or our shoes were muddy.

We didn't care if we fell and scraped our knees.

We didn't care if we looked silly trying new games or dances.

We just were.

We just belonged.

Those days, I didn't think about whether I was "good enough."

I didn't think about fitting in.

I didn't think about being judged, accepted, or compared.

I was just... me.

The kind of "me" that didn't need fixing.

The kind of "me" that didn't know what self-doubt even meant.

And that's what made leaving that place so hard.

It wasn't just about packing up rooms and furniture.

It was about packing up that fearless version of me — the kid who knew he belonged, without needing permission.

Looking back now, I realise that was the happiest kind of freedom — the freedom of not knowing yet that the world would someday expect you to be "cool", "successful", or "perfect."

Back then, just being you was enough.

And maybe that's what hurt the most when we moved.

It wasn't just about leaving a building behind.

It was about leaving a version of me behind.

A version that didn't second-guess every word.

A version that didn't think twice before running, laughing, playing, living.

The Move — And The Strange Quiet That Followed

I still remember the day we packed up that little apartment. Remember sitting on the floor of my old room.

Half my stuff was packed in brown boxes. There was this old cricket bat lying next to me—the one we all signed with coloured pens after winning our building's "World Cup."

I ran my fingers over the faded ink. The familiar walls that had echoed our laughter now stood empty, like they were mourning with me.

I sat in the middle of my messy room, surrounded by half-packed toys, broken cricket bats, and old notebooks full of doodles—and it hit me.

This wasn't just a house move.

It was a life move.

It was an ending.

And my chest felt tight in a way I didn't have words for back then.

Mom was buzzing with excitement, though.

She kept saying, "It's going to be amazing! So many kids! New friends! Swimming pool! Basketball courts! Big playgrounds! It's going to be amazing!"

You'll love it!"

And maybe it was.

Bigger house. Fancier place.

Amenities that looked like five-star resorts.

But in my heart,

It didn't feel like an upgrade.

It felt like a goodbye I wasn't ready for.

And I wanted to believe her. I really did.

She was trying so hard to make it sound like an upgrade.

When we drove into the new complex for the first time, my eyes widened. I swear it felt like stepping into a different world.

It was massive.

Towering buildings. Gleaming lobbies. Sparkling swimming pools. Cricket nets so fancy they looked like something from a movie.

Everywhere you looked, there were kids — groups of them... Kids zipping around on fancy cycles, groups already formed, laughing, playing, belonging, inside jokes already made.

I should have felt excited, right?

I should have felt like a kid stepping into Disneyland.

I should have been excited.

But instead, bro, all I felt was… small.

Tiny.

Invisible.

I missed my small, dusty cricket ground.

I missed my street dogs wagging their tails when they saw me.

I missed the old aunty handing me a cold Maaza with a smile.

I missed belonging without trying.

I missed the smell of mud and samosas.

I missed Bruno wagging his tail.

I missed playing cricket with a taped tennis ball instead of "official" tournaments with "coaches" yelling at me.

I missed belonging without having to audition for it.

That's where I think the self-doubt crept in.

Not all at once.

But slowly.

One small silence at a time.

A silence when you walk by a group and they don't notice.

A silence when you crack a joke and no one laughs.

A silence when you realise you don't know the "cool" way to wear your backpack, tie your shoelaces, or ride your cycle.

The loudest silences aren't the ones around you.

They're the ones inside you.

And inside me?

It was getting really loud.

The first few weeks were the hardest.

I tried, bro.

I really tried.

I would walk around the complex, looking at the cricket matches, the basketball games, the cycling races happening without me.

I would approach groups hesitantly, hoping to be pulled in.

One day, mustering every ounce of courage I had, I walked up to a group of boys playing tag and asked if I could join.

The boy turned, looked me straight in the eye, and said coldly,

"No. We don't want more players."

And just like that, he ran off, laughing with his friends, leaving me standing there alone.

That "no" wasn't just a rejection of playing tag.

It felt like a rejection of me.

After that day, something inside me changed.

I started expecting rejection before it even happened.

I stopped trying.

I would come back home after long, lonely walks around the complex, pretending to my mom that I had "fun" because I didn't want her to feel bad.

But inside?

I was folding into myself a little more every day.

Soon she realised I was not able to make friends here, and she would drive me daily to my old apartment in the evenings, which was far off, but still she did it for me to play with them... Life went by for a few months, but later on, things changed and they got busy, my mom got busy, and so did my self-love and not being able to mingle with the new crowd.

The Pressure Cooker

At the same time, a different kind of storm was brewing inside the house.

Everyone — family, friends, tutors, relatives — started looking at me like I was some kind of rare gem…

…but a gem that wasn't shining the way it was supposed to.

"You have SO much potential," they said.

"But you're wasting it."

"You're smart… but lazy."

"You're capable of so much more."

"If only he would just FOCUS."

"If only he realised these are his important years of opportunity — they'll never come back!"

At every family gathering, it was the same story.

Uncles, aunts, neighbours — everyone had advice.

Everyone had "suggestions" for how I could be "better."

And everyone, everyone, told my mom the same thing:

"Please encourage your son to use his full potential."

"Push him harder — don't let him settle for 50%."

"Remind him that if he doesn't take these years seriously, he'll regret it forever."

It wasn't even that they were mean.

They believed they were helping.

They believed they were cheering for me.

But to me, it felt like drowning in a sea of expectations with no life jacket in sight.

Even the tutors joined in.

"I've seen many students — he's different. He's intuitive, mature beyond his age. He notices things others miss. He remembers everything so quickly. He's a rare mind."

And while that should have made me feel proud… it didn't.

It made me feel trapped.

Because what they saw as "blessings" — I saw as a weight strapped to my shoulders.

I didn't feel like an intellectual genius.

At 16, bro, I didn't even know what "intellectual" really meant.

What was I supposed to do with that?

People described me as a "lovable child" — someone who was gentle, quiet, deeply emotional under the surface.

Someone who cared about people.

Someone who loved simplicity, honesty, calmness.

Someone who made strong emotional connections without even realising it.

And I did love those things.

I loved sitting quietly, watching the rain.

I loved late-night conversations where you talk about dreams and fears.

I loved playing with dogs, laughing till my stomach hurt, and sharing a Maaza with my friends.

I didn't want to be caught up in some mad race to "prove" myself to the world.

But the pressure kept growing.

Slowly, I started feeling like no matter what I did, it wouldn't be enough.

If I scored 80%, people asked why it wasn't 90%.

If I scored 90%, people asked why it wasn't 95%.

If I won something, people clapped — but also reminded me not to get "overconfident."

It was like standing on a treadmill that kept speeding up, and no matter how fast I ran, I couldn't keep up.

I hated that and went into a shell.

Doubt and The Silent Struggle

The pressure… it never stopped.

It followed me around like a shadow, growing longer with every passing day.

Every time I sat down to study, it wasn't just the book in front of me I was wrestling with.

It was the weight of expectations — from everyone, from myself.

And the worst part?

I couldn't talk about it.

I couldn't tell anyone how exhausted I was from trying to be something I didn't even know how to be.

I couldn't explain how every time I looked at my friends, I felt like a failure in disguise.

They seemed to have it all together — they were confident, they knew what they wanted, they were excelling at school, sports, everything.

And me?

I was standing at the sidelines, watching everyone else live their lives, wishing I could be a part of it without feeling like I had to constantly prove I deserved to be there.

And then came the self-doubt.

It wasn't loud or obvious, no dramatic meltdowns.

It was quieter, more insidious.

It whispered in my ear whenever I tried something new.

"You're not good enough."

"You'll fail, like you always do."

"Look at them — they're way ahead of you."

I remember one day sitting alone in my room, staring at the wall.

It felt like everything was falling apart.

The pressure. The expectations. That constant feeling that I was never enough, no matter how hard I tried.

I felt like a failure before I had even given myself a chance to succeed.

The problem wasn't even that I didn't want to try.

It was that I didn't know how to try anymore.

It was like I had exhausted every ounce of energy I had, trying to meet standards that didn't even belong to me.

I was running a race that wasn't mine to win…

For a long time, I thought breaking down meant I was weak. But in that silence, I started to hear myself — not the noise of what others wanted, but the quieter truth of what I needed.

Maybe I didn't have all the answers. Maybe I didn't need to.

That day didn't fix everything, but it was the first time I gave myself permission to stop running.

To sit with the mess, and still believe I was worth something.

And that was the start — not of some perfect transformation, but of learning how to carry myself through the hard days with a little more grace.

Chapter 7

Things I Never Said to My Mom

There was a time—not even that long ago—when my mom could say something as simple as "Did you eat?" and I'd instantly feel irritated. Not because she said anything wrong, but because it reminded me she was watching too closely. I hated that feeling, like I couldn't just be left alone in my own head.

She never hovered in a dramatic movie-mom way. She wasn't clingy or overbearing. But she noticed things: the tiny shifts, the change in my tone, the nights I stayed up too late, the mornings I skipped breakfast, the sighs I didn't realise were loud.

For years, I thought of her as someone I needed to protect my space from. Like I required distance to grow, and she was constantly getting in the way of that. Always checking in, always asking if I was okay, always giving me looks as if she knew something I didn't want to admit. I'd roll my eyes, say, "I'm fine," and shut the door—not because I hated her, but because I didn't know what else to do.

When I think back further, I realise this irritation had deeper roots—small childhood moments quietly building a wall I didn't even see.

Like the days when I was small, waiting by the door, counting minutes and footsteps, hoping it was finally my mom coming home. I didn't understand her job's importance back then. All I knew was the feeling of waiting—every passing minute felt like forever. I thought she chose work over me, and honestly, that felt awful.

There was also the day she accidentally slammed the door on my finger. I remember crying, calling for her, my voice shaking. I was little and scared, and the hurt wasn't just physical. She was stuck on the other side, desperately trying to open a jammed door, caught between comforting me and giving one of the biggest presentations of her career to her U.S. board. Back then, I didn't understand. I just felt angry, hurt, betrayed even.

And another time—there was water spilt on the floor, something small she probably overlooked while rushing between calls and juggling a thousand tasks. But I slipped and broke my arm. Resentment quietly built again. I silently blamed her for not noticing, for not cleaning up, for not preventing it.

I also held onto feeling smothered sometimes—the helicopter mom moments. Always watching, worrying, hovering close. As a child, it was comforting, maybe even necessary. But as I got older, it began suffocating me. I wanted independence, space, room to make mistakes without someone always nearby.

These tiny resentments piled up over the years. Without noticing, they coloured how I saw her, turning ordinary care into annoyance, simple questions into interrogation.

I assumed she couldn't really get it, that she belonged to another generation whose version of stress had nothing in common with mine. She didn't grow up with entrance exams, social media, or unspoken pressure to look like you've got it together, even when you're barely holding on. How could she understand?

But slowly—and I'm talking painfully slowly—something started to shift.

It wasn't one big moment. It was a series of tiny ones I almost missed: the way she didn't push when I said I didn't want to talk, the snack she left on my table when I skipped lunch, the way she'd sit nearby without saying anything when I paced the room, clearly spiralling.

As I grew older, I started noticing how much she showed up, despite the reasons she had to step away. Those late nights she waited up quietly, never admitting she stayed awake for me. The silent ways she checked on me, even if it felt irritating at the time.

Finally, I began to see the invisible side of her story — the quiet strength, hidden sacrifices, and silent battles she fought every day.

That's when I realised how unfair I had been, holding grudges over accidents, misunderstandings, things done out of love, even if they didn't always feel like love.

Maybe her love wasn't loud or obvious. But it was steady, always there, patiently waiting for me to notice.

One evening after the dive trip, I walked into the kitchen while she was cutting fruit—just regular fruit, papaya or something—and she looked up and asked, "How was the water?"

I almost said "fine" out of habit, but then stopped.

"It was scary," I admitted instead.

She nodded and didn't say anything for a second. Then simply: "You did it anyway."

Such a simple thing to say. No lecture, no life lesson, no "see, I told you." Just acknowledgement. It meant more than I could explain at the moment.

That night, I sat on my bed, trying to remember the last time I'd been fully honest—not polite, not technically truthful, but truly honest. The kind of honesty with no defence, no editing.

It had been a while.

Once I realised that, I thought about all the things I'd never said—not because I didn't want to, but because I didn't know how.

Like how I hated disappointing her, even if I acted like I didn't care.

Or how I sometimes wished she'd yell at me, just so I could yell back and feel something.

Or how I noticed every time she stayed up late, waiting for me to come home – even when she pretended she was just reading.

Or how part of me resented her for not being more emotional, expressive, or dramatic—until I realised that wasn't who she was.

I used to think she was emotionless because she didn't cry or explode or give dramatic rants like other moms. Now I wonder if her emotion was quieter. Steadier. Less about words and more about actions.

Like making sure I always had a full water bottle for school. Or buying my favourite cereal, even when I stopped eating it. Or memorising the names of my teachers without ever directly asking about them.

Those were her love languages. And for the longest time, I was too busy looking for bigger signs to notice.

After the maths test disaster, I expected disappointment—mine was heavy enough for both of us. But she didn't ask, "Why didn't you prepare better?" or say, "I told you this would happen." Instead, she asked quietly, "So what now?"

That question haunted me—in the best way. It was the first time I realised she wasn't trying to control me; she was trying to hand me the wheel.

Even during the friendship stuff, she never pried. She must have noticed my silence, my distant stares. Yet she never pushed. Instead, she quietly made tea in the evenings again, leaving an extra cup near mine. No forced conversation—just making space.

I didn't drink the tea. But I noticed.

When I was younger, parents seemed like background apps, managing life quietly: money, meals, messes. Now I see they're human—not superheroes, not villains—just people doing their best, while you're trying to figure yourself out.

And if you're lucky, you realise that before it's too late to say something.

One night, both of us were in the living room doing different things. She was watching something on her iPad, and I was scrolling mindlessly on my phone.

Suddenly, I said, "Hey, thanks for not freaking out when I messed up that test."

She looked up, confused at first, then smiled slightly. "I knew you'd figure it out."

No speeches. No awkward hugs. Just that. I nodded and went back to my phone, but inside, it felt like a door had opened slightly. And I didn't want to shut it again.

I'm not saying everything changed overnight. We still argue; I still roll my eyes. She still annoys me occasionally with her early morning cheeriness. But now, when she asks how I'm doing, I don't lie—not completely. I might say, "I'm tired," and actually mean it, or "Today was rough," without brushing it off.

That feels like progress.

There's a closeness that doesn't come from saying everything—it comes from being willing to say something small, consistently. Like carving a path through a forest, one step at a time.

I still don't tell her everything. Some things I'm not ready to explain; others I don't fully understand yet myself. But I don't see her as someone I have to hide from anymore.

Now I see her as someone always waiting patiently on the other side of the wall I built. Never banging on it, never trying to knock it down—just waiting. Patient, steady, quiet.

That's a different kind of strength. One I didn't respect before, but I do now.

And I've never said this—not exactly—but I'm grateful. For things she said and things she didn't. For letting me return on my own instead of dragging me out.

Maybe one day I'll say it properly. Out loud. For now, I'm starting with the basics.

I make the tea sometimes. I sit with her when she's reading. I don't flinch when she asks how I am.

It's not perfect. But it's real.

And that's enough for now.

Chapter 8

The People Who See You Before You See Yourself

Part 1

Some relationships in life don't start with fireworks or some big Instagram-worthy moment. Sometimes, they just happen — quietly, simply — like two people crossing paths at the right time, long before either of them even knows why it matters.

When I think about the people who shaped me – the ones who helped me find the pieces of myself I didn't even know were missing – I think about Mr. M.

Our bond didn't happen overnight.

There was no dramatic "mentor found!" moment.

It was built slowly, across late evening classes, half-finished math problems, awkward silences, and random conversations that somehow went way deeper than homework.

Yes, you are guessing it right — my tuition teacher, Mr. M, wasn't some IIT genius or a guy with ten degrees. He was just a regular tuition teacher —

with dusty bookshelves, no shiny projectors, and zero fancy marketing — but with this weird superpower of genuinely loving what he did.

He wasn't there to flex his resume.

He was just… there. And somehow, that was enough.

It all started when I landed in his class in Grade 11 – yeah, you guessed it right.

My mom got his name from a friend who swore he had helped a bunch of kids turn things around.

She told me, "Just give it a try. Maybe he can help you take maths and physics seriously."

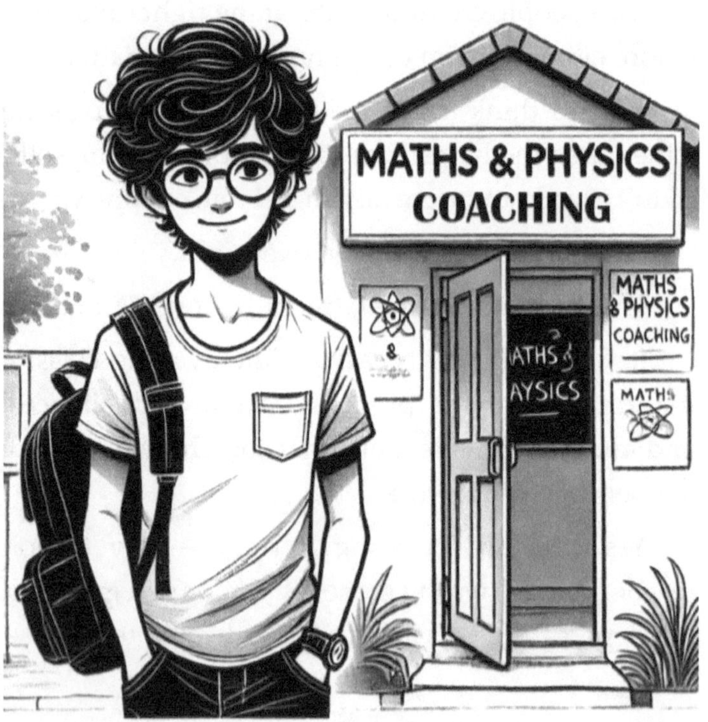

Honestly, for me, a tuition class was supposed to be that boring thing you dragged yourself to because your parents said you had to – not something that actually made you better.

But somehow, that's exactly what happened.

It wasn't planned. It wasn't some movie-style "life-changing" moment.

It just… started. Quietly. Like most important things do.

When I walked into his centre for the first time, it didn't feel anything like a "serious" place.

There were no big whiteboards, no projectors, no high-tech setups.

Just a few shelves overloaded with books, some benches and chairs, dusty windows letting in a slice of sunlight, and the heavy smell of old paper.

And then there was Mr. M.

He wasn't like any teacher I had ever met.

He didn't bark instructions.

He didn't give off that "I'm judging you" energy most teachers carry around like a badge.

He just sat there, looking at me — really looking — not to judge, not to label, but to actually see.

That first day, we didn't even open a book.

He didn't ask about my marks.

He didn't ask how many advanced placement courses I was planning to take or what colleges I was aiming for.

He asked me what I liked doing.

He asked what subjects made me curious.

He asked what made me get out of bed in the morning when I wasn't being forced to.

No one had ever asked me that before.

It was weird, honestly.

I didn't even know how to answer at first.

For so long, everything around me had been about measurements – my grades, my discipline, my structured routines, my life plans.

I had forgotten there was a version of me beyond the numbers, beyond the endless to-do lists.

Mr. M wasn't trying to fix me.

He wasn't trying to reprogram me into some "ideal student" model.

He was just... helping me remember who I was when I wasn't trying so hard to be someone else.

He made me realise that learning wasn't about cramming or copying formulas.

It was about understanding my own style – what made me curious, what made me stubborn, what made me tick.

And, bro, that changed everything.

Of course, at first, I resisted.

Old habits die hard.

I showed up late.

I cracked dumb jokes to avoid answering tough questions.

I acted like it didn't matter.

But Mr. M never raised his voice.

Never guilt-tripped me.

Never made me feel like a disappointment.

He just kept showing up.

And little by little, so did I.

Not because I had to.

Not because someone was forcing me.

But because, for the first time in a long time, I actually wanted to.

At first, he was just another adult trying to teach me things I wasn't sure I even cared about.

But over time, it shifted.

He became someone who got it.

Someone who saw the version of me I wanted to be seen.

We weren't just solving equations or prepping for exams.

We were talking about life.

About dreams.

About doubts we didn't know how to say out loud.

About how figuring yourself out doesn't happen on a schedule.

What started off feeling like random catch-up conversations turned into something bigger —the kind of bigger that makes you realise the invisible fingerprints people leave on your life, without even trying.

"Mr. M wasn't just a tutor—he was a mentor, a guide, and at times, even a friend who saw potential in me when I struggled to see it myself."

He was someone who reminded you to look up once in a while—to not just solve problems on paper, but to pay attention to the quiet, complicated, stubborn human being you already were.

He taught connection before correction.

He taught patience before precision.

He taught showing up – not just to class, but for yourself.

It wasn't like one day I magically transformed.

It was slow.

Messy.

Real.

Somewhere between bad jokes, half-solved problems, and endless "one more try" moments, he made me focus—not by scaring me, but by making me care.

Focus wasn't about sitting still.

It was about being present.

It was about staying with something long enough to understand it—even if it made you uncomfortable.

That's what Mr. M had been teaching me all along, without ever once saying it out loud.

You don't win because you're perfect.

You win because you stay.

You stay when it's boring.

You stay when it's hard.

You stay when your mind whispers it's easier to quit.

You stay for yourself.

I still remember the day I took my SAT maths exam.

I walked out of the centre with zero hesitation, and called Mr. M immediately, grinning from ear to ear.

"Sir, it's 800 on 800. Just telling you early so no surprises later."

Yeah, it's me – the same kid who used to bluff through algebra worksheets,

the kid who thought gaming strategies mattered more than geometry proofs,

the kid who secretly thought he wasn't built for "smart kid" stuff.

That kid.

I did it.

But honestly?

The 800 wasn't the real win.

The real win was not quitting on myself.

It was the fact that even when I zoned out, even when I messed up, even when I doubted everything – I kept coming back.

And now here I am – all set to take on my Grade 11 Maths exams this May. ☺

Part 2

Recently, I sat down with Mr. M to talk about our journeys. We ended up covering way more than I expected – our struggles, our growth, our definitions of success, and the invisible ways we've left fingerprints on each other's lives without even realising it.

At the heart of it all was someone who connected with me in an unexpected way – a tuition teacher named Mr. M.

He wasn't just another teacher drilling me in physics or maths. He showed me that real learning isn't about memorising formulas – it's about remembering who you are, even when the world tries to make you forget.

Mr. M had an interesting journey himself. He started out as a gym trainer, chasing a passion most people around him didn't really understand. Later, he switched to teaching – not because it was easier (it wasn't), but because he knew kids like me needed someone to believe in us. That path wasn't smooth; he battled his own insecurities, trying to become the kind of person who could lift others up even when he wasn't always sure how to lift himself.

Hearing his story was eye-opening. It made me realise that every confident person you meet has a backstory you don't see – one full of stumbles, hesitations, and getting back up even when the ground feels shaky under their feet.

We laughed about how life sometimes throws the right people at you without warning. It's not always about finding the *perfect* mentor or friend; often it's about two imperfect journeys colliding at just the right time – and somehow, that ends up being perfect enough.

At one point, Mr. M smiled and said, "You're the hero of your story, bro." I burst out laughing because, honestly, some days, I still feel like I'm barely holding it together. But maybe that's what growing up is – starting to believe the good things that people already see in you.

Later, he shared a memory from when I first joined his class that honestly surprised me.

He told me that when I first joined his class, he thought I was… well, kind of dumb. Not because I couldn't get the answers, but because I kept asking the same questions over and over. At first, it annoyed him, but over time, he realised I wasn't being slow or careless — I was actually trying to understand. Not to memorise, not to fake it, but to actually *get it*.

Hearing that perspective made me grin and think hard. That stubborn persistence of mine – that need to dig until something made sense – wasn't a flaw after all. It was actually a quiet kind of strength. It clicked for me that struggling doesn't mean you're failing; more often, it just means you're trying harder than most people would.

We went on to talk about what success really means. For both of us, that definition has changed over time. Once, success was all about grades, trophies, and pats on the back. Now, it's about showing up when it matters and being someone others can rely on. It's about valuing kindness over applause and consistency over recognition.

Mr. M told me that over the years, he's learned to take more time to understand people instead of rushing to conclusions. I realised I've learned that from him too – one of those small lessons hidden between all the bigger ones.

We even discussed how hard it is to balance being a teacher and being a friend. Mr. M said that meeting students like me has changed him as well. He learned that teaching isn't about handing out answers; it's about instilling belief. It's not about saying, "Here's the formula," but rather, "You're someone who figures things out."

One of the many moments that stayed with both of us wasn't about academics at all and had nothing to do with textbooks. One that stood out was a day trip to Mandi – a day full of laughter, simple conversations, and the kind of bonding that doesn't need big words. We also remembered a random memory that made both of us smile — an ice cream outing where we ended up mixing two weird drinks just for fun, laughing like little kids without caring about how grown up we were supposed to be.

It's strange – the moments that stick with you usually aren't the ones you plan. They're the ones where you're completely present – unguarded, unapologetic, alive. Those unplanned experiences made me realise something: real mentors don't sugarcoat everything. They're the ones who challenge you when you want to quit, call you out when you're hiding behind fear, and keep believing in you – loudly and stubbornly – even when you're whispering doubts to yourself.

As our conversation was winding down, it shifted back to me. And honestly, while I know I still have a long journey ahead – no grand plan and no perfect checklist – what matters is that two people, both still figuring it out, crossed paths at the right time.

And maybe that's the real win. Not the perfect score. Not the certificate.

Not the big speech.

If there's one thing I've learned from Mr. M, it's that real growth doesn't happen just because someone pushes you from the outside. It happens when someone quietly believes in you, until you start believing in yourself – and then you begin to push yourself. And it doesn't happen perfectly or all at once. It happens slowly and steadily, at your own messy, imperfect pace.

You don't need the loudest cheers or a shelf full of trophies. Sometimes, one person who truly sees you, even while you're still struggling to see yourself, is enough. That one person can make you feel – without ever saying it outright – that *you're already enough. Now imagine how far you can go.* And bro, when you have even one person like that, you're already halfway there.

That truth was simple: the best parts of who we become are often shaped by those who believed in us before we believed in ourselves. After all, it often takes someone else's faith – someone who sees your potential before you do – to reveal the quiet strengths you've had inside you all along.

This isn't the end of my story.

It's just where I finally started seeing myself for who I really am – not the guy trying to fit in, not the guy weighed down by expectations, but the guy who's figuring it out, one messy, determined step at a time. Growing emotionally has changed not only how I see myself, but also how I approach all the things I used to try to shortcut. Somewhere along the way, I realised that all those small choices – studying, practising, showing up – are part of the bigger story I'm writing about myself. It isn't just about passing exams anymore; it's about who I'm becoming when no one else is watching.

Chapter 9

Shortcut Season Is Over

I used to be the king of shortcuts.

Not in a shady, cheat-on-the-test kind of way. More like—I could make anything seem effortless, even when I was barely holding it together. I was the guy who studied five minutes before the quiz and still managed to scrape a decent grade. The guy who Googled "summary of Macbeth" five minutes before English class and threw around big words like "tragic flaw" and "dramatic irony" like I actually knew what I was talking about.

I took pride in it, honestly. There's something addictive about getting away with doing less. Especially when people still think you've got it under control.

But it wasn't just school. I realised, somewhere along the way, I'd started using shortcuts in pretty much every part of my life.

Feel overwhelmed? Pretend I'm fine.

Feel hurt? Make a joke, walk away.

Feel scared? Do something else and call it "not my thing."

I had shortcuts for emotions. For conversations. For relationships. For dealing with teachers, parents, even myself.

And for a while, it worked. No one questioned me. I didn't question myself. I got by.

But here's the thing about shortcuts: they save you time until they don't.

When everything in my life started spiralling—the test I bombed, the friend group that ghosted me, the weight of everything I wasn't saying—I suddenly didn't have anything to fall back on. All the tricks that used to work just stopped working. And it hit me: I wasn't ahead. I was lost.

After the maths test, when I finally admitted I needed more time and asked to delay the exam, it was the first time I chose *not* to shortcut something. It wasn't a big, dramatic decision. I just didn't want to feel like a fraud anymore. I wanted to *try*—not pretend.

That decision changed me more than I expected.

I started studying—not just scrolling through summaries or asking friends to explain stuff at the last minute, but actually sitting down, opening the book, and working through the problems. It was slow. It was boring. It was frustrating. But it also felt… real. Like I was building something for the first time instead of borrowing it from someone else.

The weird part? I didn't hate it.

I mean, I didn't suddenly love maths. But I liked how it made me feel to show up every day and try. No shortcuts. No skipping steps. Just effort. Consistent, honest effort.

There's something weirdly satisfying about doing the hard thing and knowing you did it the hard way. Like, even if you don't get it perfect, you earn whatever result comes.

That feeling started spilling into other parts of my life as well.

I started sleeping on time—not because I suddenly became super disciplined, but because I noticed how much better I felt the next day when I wasn't running on fumes.

I started showing up to class prepared—not out of fear, but because it felt better than bluffing my way through another lesson.

It wasn't perfect. Some days I still wanted to take the easy way out. I still had moments where I thought, "Ugh, what's the point?" But the difference now was that I could hear that voice in my head and not listen to it. Or at least not *always* listen to it.

One afternoon, I was sitting at my desk trying to solve this ridiculously complicated math problem. I must've redone the same step three times and kept getting it wrong. The old me would have given up and Googled the answer. But I didn't. I sat there, annoyed and twitchy, muttering to myself, and kept trying.

When I finally got it—like actually figured it out without help—I didn't shout or fist pump or anything. I just sat back, breathed, and smiled a little.

Because that feeling? That was mine. I hadn't borrowed it. I hadn't faked it. I'd *earned* it.

There's this lie we're sold—especially in school, especially online—that the smartest people are the ones who don't have to try. That effort is embarrassing. That caring too much makes you uncool.

I believed that for a long time. I thought caring was a weakness. That if I tried and failed, it would prove I wasn't good enough.

But now I see it differently. Trying doesn't mean you're weak. It means you're brave enough to care. And failing doesn't mean you suck – it just means you're learning.

Once I understood that, the shortcuts started to lose their appeal. They felt small. Lazy. Shallow. And I didn't want to be small or shallow anymore. I wanted to be *real*—even if it meant messing up sometimes.

It wasn't just about academics. It was about how I showed up everywhere.

I started being more honest with my mom too. Not about everything—I wasn't suddenly spilling my deepest fears over dinner—but I stopped pretending so much. If I was anxious, I didn't lie. That alone changed our conversations completely.

And when I caught myself reaching for a shortcut—like saying "I'm good" when I wasn't, or brushing off a mistake instead of owning it—I paused. Not always. But enough to start rewiring how I responded to things.

There's something powerful about choosing the harder thing and watching yourself handle it.

So yeah – shortcut season is over.

Not because I've become this ultra-mature, disciplined, perfect person. I still procrastinate. I still get lazy. I still want to bail on hard stuff sometimes. But now, I catch myself. And I choose differently, more often than not.

Because the long way – the harder way – is where the real stuff happens.

Where you figure out what you're made of.

When you realise that the version of you who *tries* is way more interesting than the one who fakes it.

And honestly? I'd rather be interesting than impressive.

Chapter 10

Slow Wins, Soft Strength

If you'd met me a year ago, you probably would have described me as "chill."

That was the vibe I gave off—relaxed, unbothered, just floating through life with a kind of casual confidence. And honestly, I believed it. I thought that being chill meant I had things under control. That if I didn't panic, didn't push, didn't care too much, I was winning.

Now I think I just didn't want to feel too much.

Because when you care—even a little—it opens the door to disappointment, failure, awkwardness, and all the other feelings I spent most of my life trying to avoid.

But here's what I've learned: caring quietly might be the bravest thing you can do.

Not the loud, motivational kind of caring. Not the "I'm gonna change the world!" kind. I mean the soft kind. The day-to-day kind. The kind where you show up, even when no one's watching. Even when you don't feel like it. Even when you're not sure it's working.

That kind of strength isn't flashy. It doesn't get applause. But it's real.

And for me, it started with small things.

Like waking up on time—not because someone forced me to, but because I wanted my mornings to feel less chaotic.

Like finishing an assignment early and *not* bragging about it.

Like helping someone without screenshotting it for proof.

None of this was impressive. None of it made me stand out. But it made me feel grounded in a way I never had before. Like I was living from the inside out, not from the outside in.

I stopped waiting for life to feel dramatic in order for it to feel meaningful.

The slow wins started adding up.

There was this one evening when I finished a full week of school without skipping a single task. That had never happened before—not because I was lazy, but because I always found ways to cut corners. But this week? I did it all. Showed up. Stayed present. Crossed things off without making a big deal about it.

At the end of the week, I didn't reward myself with a new gadget or a binge session. I just went out for a walk, no headphones, and let myself feel proud. No hype-posting proud. Just that quiet, internal nod you give yourself when you know you're doing better—even if no one else notices.

That kind of pride hits differently.

And it made me realise how much I used to chase the loud stuff—the quick laughs, the validation, the external praise. It's not like those things are bad. But they're temporary. They fade fast. What sticks is the feeling you get when you keep promises to yourself. When you become someone you trust.

That was new to me.

For a long time, I didn't trust myself. I said I'd do things and didn't. I said I was fine when I wasn't. I said I didn't care when I cared a lot. That gap between who I said I was and who I actually was? It messed with my head more than I realised.

But now, that gap is smaller.

I still mess up. I still procrastinate. I still have days where I want to ghost everyone and lie in bed watching pointless videos. But more often than not, I pull myself back. Not with guilt or pressure—just with patience.

Because I know now that growth isn't a straight line. It loops and stutters and doubles back. You don't level up all at once. You level up quietly, in the background, on days when nothing big happens.

It shows up when you choose to respond differently to the same old trigger.

When you sit with your feelings instead of pushing them away.

When you ask for help, even though your pride says you shouldn't.

When you give someone grace, not because they deserve it, but because you remember what it's like to mess up and still want another chance.

I don't always get it right, but I try.

And trying is no longer something I'm embarrassed about.

I used to think effort was cringeworthy. Like if you had to work hard, it meant you weren't naturally good enough. But now I see effort as a kind of love—for yourself, for your goals, for your future. It's saying, "I'm not perfect, but I care enough to keep showing up."

That shift changed everything.

In school, I'm still not topping the charts. But I understand what I'm learning. I ask better questions. I'm not scared to say "I don't know" because I know it doesn't define me—it just describes where I am right now.

With friends, things are still weird sometimes. I'm not back in the group chat. I'm not part of every plan. But I've reconnected with a couple of people—quietly, without drama. Just checking in. Just being there. And that's enough for now.

With my mom, things feel different in a good way. We don't have deep talks every night. But we have a rhythm now. We eat together more often. She tells me about her work, and I actually listen. I tell her when I'm overwhelmed, and she actually listens too.

It's not a "perfect relationship." It's a real one.

And most importantly, with myself? I'm no longer avoiding everything.

I'm not scared of the quiet. Or the stillness. Or the uncertainty.

Okay—that's a lie. I *am* scared sometimes. But I don't run from it the same way. I let it sit with me. I write about it. I walk it off. I do the math problem. I take a deep breath. I send the awkward message.

I don't try to fix everything at once.

I just try to do the next right thing.

That's what slow strength looks like. Not powering through. Not pretending you're fine. But staying in it, even when it's uncomfortable.

That kind of strength is quiet and soft. But it's mine.

And I'm learning to trust it.

Part 4

Turning the Page

(Trying again, on my own terms.)

Chapter 11

I Didn't Mean to Start Anything

It started with books.

Not some deep, symbolic moment—just a pile of old textbooks gathering dust on my shelf. My mom had asked me to clear them out before school started again. I was in one of those post-study moods where you want to do something mindless, so I started sorting.

I found my old science book from eighth grade. The one with diagrams I'd drawn in the margins and random notes like "Ask Sir about pH scale" that I clearly never followed up on. I almost tossed it, but something about the scribbles made me stop.

I sat on the floor and flipped through it for a while. It wasn't nostalgia exactly—more like this strange feeling of distance. Like I couldn't believe there was a time when *this* was my biggest problem.

Later that evening, over dinner, my mom mentioned that our house help's son had scored well in his board exams. "He used the books we gave them last year," she added, almost as an afterthought.

That stuck with me.

It wasn't like we had donated some huge library or anything. Just a few old books we didn't need anymore. But hearing that they'd actually helped someone—that some kid had flipped through those pages and maybe struggled, maybe succeeded, maybe underlined stuff the same way I had—it hit differently.

I didn't say much that night, but I kept thinking about it.

The next morning, I told my mom, "Let's give away all my old storybooks, toys, and unused stuff to someone who can use them."

Mom was thrilled. Knowing her enthusiasm, I quickly added - "Let's keep it small. I'll ask my friends too, but let's not overdo it."

I started small. I texted a couple of people in my class, asking if they had books they didn't need. Some replied. Most didn't. But the ones who did offered more than I expected—bags of books!

And Just Like That… Dhara Life Was Born 

An idea turned into a name. A feeling turned into a platform.

Dhara Life began with one simple thought: "We all have something to give. Let's just start with that."

I wanted to create something that allowed more people—kids like me—to make a lasting difference.

We started with a book donation drive.

We collected over 700 books and built a mini-library for a government school close to where we stayed.

The smiles on those kids' faces when they opened the books? #Unmatched.

It felt... good. Not "heroic" or "noble." Just simple and useful.

I didn't think of it as "starting something." I wasn't trying to build a movement. I just thought, if this small thing helped one person, maybe it could help another.

- We Didn't Stop There. We kept going!
- Storytelling sessions for younger kids in the school.
- Weekend classes to help kids with maths.
- Posters placed in schools before the exam season, saying No to stress about exams.
- A mini robotics workshop with help from my U.S. friends to spark creativity and innovation among kids.

Every new effort reminded me – you don't need to be big to do something big.

The first time a kid from the government school came up to me and said, "I really liked the science book. Do you have the next one?" —I nearly choked on my response. Not because I didn't have it (I did), but because I couldn't believe someone saw me as someone who *had* something to offer.

It was the first time I felt useful in a way that didn't depend on grades, popularity, being funny, or chill. Just useful because I showed up and did something that mattered, however small.

That changed me more than anything else.

Because once you know what it feels like to matter—to someone, to something—you start craving that feeling more than validation or likes or high-fives.

You start doing things for the sake of doing them.

Not because they're easy. Not because someone told you to. But because they light something up in you that shortcuts never could.

The Water Plant: A Dream, A Drive, and a Big Win 💧

One day, the school principal mentioned that the kids didn't have clean drinking water.

That just didn't sit right with me. I didn't know how or where to start, but I knew we had to try.

I'd read somewhere that in some parts of the country, students dropped out of school during the summer months because the walk to get water was too long. I didn't know if that was true everywhere, but it sounded astounding. Like, how does a problem that basic still exist?

So I started asking questions. Where do people get water? How often? Is it clean? Is it safe?

Most of the answers were vague or too complicated for me to fully understand. But one thing was clear—access to clean water wasn't guaranteed, even in places that seemed okay on the surface.

I then thought of a fundraiser campaign. I called friends, family, cousins—anyone who could help. And with a lot of support, we installed a water purification plant in that school.

From the start to the end, i.e. from deciding to run a campaign to installing the plant, all through it, one thing stayed the same: it felt good to care.

Not in a "look-at-me" way. Just in a quiet, steady way. Like I was using my brain for.

I didn't post about Dhara Life on Instagram. I didn't add it to my bio or turn it into some startup story. I still don't know what it's supposed to be. Maybe it'll grow. Maybe it'll fade out. But it doesn't matter.

What matters is that I tried.

That I saw a gap and stepped into it. That I paid attention to the world outside my bubble. That I stopped asking, "What's the least I can do?" and started wondering, "What would happen if I just did this one small thing?"

That mindset shift - That's the real growth.

I realised that I often thought giving back meant sacrificing. But really, it means sharing from what you already have. Even the tiniest acts of kindness can create ripples far beyond what we imagine.

Chapter 12

I'm Not Done Yet
(But I'm Different Now)

It's funny how nothing looks different on the outside.

My room's still the same. Same desk. Same creaky chair. Same hoodie draped over the back of it like I'm too lazy to fold it (which I am). My textbooks are still stacked messily in the corner, and my to-do list is still half lies. The house sounds the same. The school bell rings the same. My friends post the same filtered pictures with the same tired captions.

And yet, something feels different. Not everything. But me.

I didn't wake up one day and decide to change. I didn't burn the old version of myself or make a grand announcement. I didn't get a new haircut or suddenly turn into someone who drinks green smoothies and wakes up at 5 a.m.

What happened was quieter.

It was one small moment after another. Choosing to show up when I didn't want to. Saying how I felt when I didn't know if it would land. Facing things I would've avoided before—not perfectly, but without running. Staying with the discomfort instead of trying to dodge it. And somewhere in the middle of all of that, I realised I was becoming someone I liked a little more.

Not someone impressive. Just someone real.

There's this pressure, especially when you're a teenager, to have some kind of identity locked in. Like you're supposed to pick your path early and stick to it. Be the smart one. Or the funny one. Or the sporty one. Or the kid who doesn't care about any of it and just vibes through life.

But what no one tells you is that most of us are still figuring out how we even feel on a random Tuesday.

And maybe that's okay.

I used to think that if I didn't know who I was, that meant something was wrong with me. That I was behind. That everyone else had some kind of inner compass while I was just spinning.

I used to think effort was cringeworthy. Like if you had to work hard, it meant you weren't naturally good enough. But now I see effort as a kind of love—for yourself, for your goals, for your future. It's saying, "I'm not perfect, but I care enough to keep showing up."

Now I think—maybe not knowing is part of becoming.

I'm still figuring stuff out. Like how to be consistent without being hard on myself. How to forgive people who never apologised. How to be okay with friendships that drift without needing to make them villains in my head.

I'm still learning how to rest without guilt. How to care deeply without turning that into pressure. How to feel things without labelling them as weakness.

I'm still working on speaking up when I need help, instead of waiting for someone to guess.

I'm still trying to remember that not everything needs to be a turning point—some things can just happen, be felt, and move on.

There's no big win I'm ending this book with. No final transformation scene. No "and that's how I found my purpose" paragraph.

I didn't become a new person. I just stopped pretending to be the old one.

That version of me—the one who coasted, avoided, joked his way through everything—he's still here. But he doesn't drive anymore. He's in the back seat, eating chips and occasionally yelling dumb things. I let him be there. But I don't let him steer.

And now? I've started paying attention to a quieter voice. The one that says, "You can do hard things." The one that says, "Try again." The one that says, "Take your time, but don't disappear."

I'm not always good at listening to it, but I know it's there now.

That changes everything.

I still mess up. I still overthink texts. I still get tired of trying. But I don't give up as quickly. I don't bail on myself at the first sign of failure. I sit with it. Sometimes I write about it. Sometimes I just let it pass.

There's this thing I heard someone say once: "You're allowed to be a work in progress and still be proud of who you are."

That's how I feel now.

I'm not done. But I'm proud. Not because I have everything figured out – but because I stayed with myself through the parts I didn't.

And the truth is, I'm not writing this as a message to anyone else.

I'm writing it because maybe one day, I'll forget again. Maybe I'll go through another week where I feel lost, or invisible, or like everything is spiralling again. And when that happens, I want to be able to look back and remember:

You've been here before.

You got through it.

You didn't have a map, but you made it anyway.

And you didn't do it all at once—you did it in pieces. In pages. In pauses. In moments when it didn't look like progress, but it was.

So if you're reading this and expecting some big answer – I don't have one.

But I can tell you this: if something in you is stirring, if you're questioning things you used to be sure about, if you're tired of pretending everything's fine…

That doesn't mean you're broken.

It means you're paying attention.

And maybe—just maybe—you're not falling apart.

Maybe you're unfolding.

I'm still figuring it out – the mistakes, the doubts, the dreams.

But for the first time, I'm not scared of it.

I'm actually kind of excited to see where this messy, unpredictable journey takes me next.

Because maybe figuring it out isn't a one-time thing.

Maybe it's just the best part of the whole ride.

Letter to My 13-Year-Old Self

Yo.

I know you're probably sitting on your bed right now with your phone in one hand, acting like nothing bothers you, but feeling weird for some reason you can't explain. Let me save you some time – you're not crazy. You're just overwhelmed and don't have the words for it yet.

So, a few things you should know. Not "wise" things. Just stuff I wish someone had told me before I learned it the hard way.

First: **You don't need to act like you've got it all figured out.** No one does. Literally everyone is faking it. Some people are just better at pretending than others.

Second: **Being chill isn't a personality.** You're not weak for caring about stuff. You don't have to laugh everything off. You're allowed to feel stuff and still be okay.

Also, stop thinking your friends are going to stay the same forever. Some will drift. Some will be weird. Some will hurt you and not even realise it. That sucks, yeah. But it's not the end of the world. You'll find your people—and you'll become better at being one of those people too.

Oh, and you know how you're avoiding everything hard by joking, quitting early, or pretending it doesn't matter?

Yeah… that stops working eventually.

Start doing stuff even if it's uncomfortable. Especially if it's uncomfortable. That's where the good stuff is. And I don't mean big heroic stuff. I mean the tiny things—asking questions in class, admitting when you messed up, texting someone first, actually studying for real. Start there.

One last thing—and this might sound lame, but whatever: **you're not falling behind.** You're growing in ways you won't even notice until later. The stuff you think makes you different, slower, or less confident? That's exactly the stuff that's gonna make you stronger.

So, take a deep breath.

Also… drink more water.

You're weirdly bad at that.

You're doing better than you think.

Acknowledgements

People, Bots & Books That Got Me Here

First, thanks to the people who showed up – even when I wasn't always easy to show up for.

Thanks to my mom — whether she was nagging me or giving me space (usually the first ☺), she played a major role in my life… from the late-night pep talks to the quiet strength she never stops showing.

Thanks to my friends (you know who you are) – the ones who stuck around even when life got weird, silent, or chaotic.

Thanks to all the quiet people who taught me small things without even knowing it – you're part of this story too.

Thanks to Supriya ma'am, for helping me structure the book and probably seeing it coming before I even did. Your support kept me sane.

Thanks to Mr. M for seeing me before I saw myself and for teaching me that some wins aren't about scores – they're about staying.

To everyone who shaped these experiences – friends, teachers, mentors, family – whether directly or silently, thank you for being part of my story.

To every book I've read and every character I've fallen in love with — thank you for messing with my emotions, making me believe in stories, and reminding me that a messy, imperfect story is still worth telling.

To ChatGPT—yes, the AI—thanks for never saying "this is a bad idea" at 2 a.m., and for answering questions even when I had no clue what I was doing.

And finally, to all the weird, wonderful, awkward, and eye-roll-worthy experiences I've had as a 16-year-old – thanks for the content. Wouldn't trade it. (Well, maybe one or two things.)

And to the version of myself that kept writing, even when it felt easier to stop – thank you too.

This book isn't perfect. Neither am I.

But maybe that's exactly the point.